Sailor Moo
Cow at Sea

story by
LISA WHEELER

Sailor

pictures by
PONDER GOEMBEL

Moo
Cow at Sea

A RICHARD JACKSON BOOK
ATHENEUM BOOKS *for* YOUNG READERS
NEW YORK LONDON TORONTO SYDNEY SINGAPORE

Atheneum Books for Young Readers
An imprint of Simon & Schuster Children's Publishing Division
1230 Avenue of the Americas
New York, New York 10020

Text copyright © 2002 by Lisa Wheeler
Illustrations copyright © 2002 by Ponder Goembel

Book design by Michael Nelson
The text of this book is set in CooperBT.
The illustrations are rendered in acrylic paint.

Printed in Hong Kong
2 4 6 8 10 9 7 5 3 1

LIBRARY OF CONGRESS CATALOGING-IN-PUBLICATION DATA
Wheeler, Lisa, 1963–
Sailor Moo: cow at sea / written by Lisa Wheeler ; illustrated by Ponder Goembel.
p.   cm.
"A Richard Jackson Book."
ISBN 0-689-84219-8
1. Cows—Juvenile poetry. 2. Ocean travel—Juvenile poetry. 3. Children's poetry, American.
[1. Cows—Poetry. 2. American poetry.] I. Goembel, Ponder, ill. II. Title.
PS3573.H4329 S25 2002
811/.6—dc21   00-066386

FIRST
EDITION

For my daughter, Katie,
who moo-ved me to write this book. . . . .
and with special thanks to Karma,
who prodded me to finish it.
—L. W.

To my mother who,
like Moo's, has seen her daughter
off into the world.
—P. G.

All year long, the dairy cows
would stand . . . and graze . . . and chew.
They truly were contented cows—
except for little Moo.

Moo watched the field of waving wheat,
and wished for ocean swells.
She sniffed the freshness of the grass,
but wished for ocean smells.

Soon, Moo grew tired of dreaming dreams,
and said farewell one day.
She packed her bucket and her bell,
then hoofed it toward the bay.

Yo~ho~ho
And a shiver~me~be
Whoever heard of a cow at sea?

Moo climbed aboard the nearest ship—
a feline fishing boat,
owned by Captain Silver Claw,
a tom with cindered coat.

High atop his lofty perch
the whiskered captain towered.
"If ye be yellow, get off now!"
But Moo was not a coward.

She looked the captain in the eye,
and said, "Here's what I'll do.
Fresh milk each day will pay my way.
Just call me Sailor Moo."

Then Silver Claw, he licked his jaw
and rubbed his trusty hook.
"One brimming pail each day you sail.
You'll be our galley cook."

Yo-ho-ho
And a shiver-me-be
Sailor Moo has gone to sea!

Moo loved the way the ocean sang.
"Like moo-sic," she would utter,
as rocking, rolling ocean waves
would churn her milk to butter.

She couldn't speak the language
of the spitting, hissing crew.
They'd laugh and joke like feline folk,
ignoring Sailor Moo.

So Moo befriended ocean life.
She loved the manatee.
She'd moo and low. They'd swim below—
her cousins of the sea!

Then came one day, near Hogshead Bay,
a sudden, savage gale.
Poor Sailor Moo, into the brew,
was tossed head over tail.

Yo~ho~ho
And a shiver~me~be
Sailor Moo is lost at sea!

Within the swell, she rang her bell.
The sea cows heard her chime.
Too near the reef! They dived beneath
and saved her just in time.

They swam her to the nearest ship,
a crusty cattle barge.
Red Angus, handsome brawny bull,
appeared to be in charge.

Then Sailor Moo, with much ado,
was ushered on the deck,
where cows and steers with studded ears
wore scarves around their necks.

Red Angus bowed, addressed the crowd,
"We welcome Moo on board!"
Who was this crew? She had no clue—
a bovine pirate horde!

Yo-ho-ho
And a shiver-me-be
Pirate cows be out at sea!

Poor Moo was shocked the day she walked
into the pirate's lair.
She saw rare jewels and milking stools
among the treasures there.

Moo's heart was pure, so she was sure
it must be a mistake.
Looting steers? Cow buccaneers?
She felt her stomachs ache . . .

. . . and with a sigh, "Angus! Why?"
Then neither said a word.
Moo knew the truth. She saw the proof!
He led this lawless herd.

Red Angus gazed into her eyes.
His heart began to warm.
In Moo he'd seen his dairy queen
and now he must reform.

Yo-ho-ho
And a shiver-me-be
Moo finds romance out at sea!

The bull gave up his pirate ways,
forsook the pirate life.
He said *adieu* to ship and crew—
and Moo became his wife.

Sailor Moo, content at last—
she couldn't want for more.
No need to roam, she makes her home
along the Jersey shore.

They have a bonny baby now,
a sweet, cream-colored calf.
Part Sailor Moo, part Angus, too—
they call her Half-'n'-half!

Yo~ho~ho
And a shiver~me~be
Happily ever after three!